Little Ones Do!

BY Jana Novotny Hunter

ILLUSTRATED BY Sally Anne Lambert

DUTTON CHILDREN'S BOOKS · NEW YORK

When Daddy's snore, snore, snoring,
And Mommy's sleepy, too . . .
A Little One helps
them both wake up,
Because that's what
Little Ones do!

All together, one, two, three . . .
Roly-poly, tickle-tum,
Lift the blankie — boo!

Again and again till Daddy says,
"It's breakfast time for you!"

When Mommy's rush, rush, rushing,
And Daddy's hurrying, too . . .
A Little One goes . . . a little . . .
  more . . . sl-o-wwwly,

Because
that's what
Little Ones do!

All together, one, two, three . . .
Have a race to wash, wash face,

Get dressed,
Pull on vest,
Say, "Peekaboo!"

Brush your hair and
fetch your bear.

Now Little One's
ready to go!

When Daddy's car *brrmm-brrmms* away,
And Mommy's leaving, too . . .

A Little One watches and waves bye-bye,
Because that's what Little Ones do!

So join in all together, one, two, three!
Blow bubbles, soap bubbles,
Catch a floaty rainbow—pop!

Have fun playing all day long,
Until it's time to stop.

Then Little Ones look at books,
And Big Ones look at them, too . . .

And families come to pick them up,
Because that's what families do!

Home together, one, two, three . . . .
Roly-poly, ride the pony,
Faster, faster—"Wheeee!"

Round and round the living room,
"You can't catch me!"

Then Daddy's puff, puff, puffing,
And Mommy needs to rest . . .

So a Little One sings
them a bedtime song,
Because that's what
Little Ones do best!

La-la-la!

All together, one, two, three . . .
Kiss, kiss, snuggle, snuggle,
Hug each other tight.
Tuck in cozy under blankie
And say good night!